Tiger-Tiger, Is It True?

Four questions to make you smile again

Byron Katie
and
Hans Wilhelm

Illustrated by Hans Wilhelm

HAY HOUSE, INC.
Carlsbad, California • New York City
London • Sydney • Johannesburg
Vancouver • New Delhi

Published and distributed in the United States by: Hay House, Inc.: www.hayhouse.com • *Published and distributed in Australia by:* Hay House Australia Pty. Ltd.: www.hayhouse.com.au • *Published and distributed in the United Kingdom by:* Hay House UK, Ltd.: www.hayhouse.co.uk • *Published and distributed in the Republic of South Africa by:* Hay House SA (Pty), Ltd.: www.hayhouse.co.za • *Distributed in Canada by:* Raincoast Books: www.raincoast.com • *Published in India by:* Hay House Publishers India: www.hayhouse .co.in

Design: Amy Gingery • *Illustrations:* © Hans Wilhelm

Library of Congress Control Number: 2009924000

ISBN: 978-1-4019-2560-4
Digital ISBN: 978-1-4019-2680-9

15 14 13 12 11 10 9
1st edition, November 2009

Printed in the United States of America

SUSTAINABLE FORESTRY INITIATIVE
Certified Chain of Custody
Promoting Sustainable Forestry
www.sfiprogram.org
SFI-01268
SFI label applies to the text stock

A Note from Byron Katie

I am delighted that you have opened this book about my little friend Tiger-Tiger and his problems. Freedom is always just a question away.

The Work, which forms the basis of this story, is a way to identify and question the thoughts that cause all the suffering in the world. It is a way to find peace with yourself and with the world. The old, the young, the sick, the well, the educated, the uneducated—anyone with an open mind can do this Work.

Those of you who are interested in learning how to do The Work, yourselves or with your children, will find everything you need to know in my book *Loving What Is,* or on my Website: **www.thework.com**.

Since the beginning of time, people have been trying to change the world so that they can be happy. This hasn't ever worked, because it approaches the problem backward. What The Work gives us is a way to change the projector—mind—rather than the projected. It's like when there's a piece of lint on a projector's lens. We think there's a flaw on the screen, and we try to change this person and that person, whomever the flaw appears to be on next. But it's futile to try to change the projected images. Once we realize where the lint is, we can clear the lens itself. This is the end of suffering, and the beginning of a little joy in paradise.

The Four Questions and Turnaround

1. Is it true?

2. Can you absolutely know that it's true?

3. How do you react, what happens, when you believe that thought?

4. Who would you be without the thought?

   and

Turn it around, then find at least three specific, genuine examples of how the turnaround is true in your life.

Now let's see what happens to Tiger-Tiger.

Katie

One morning, Tiger-Tiger got out of bed on the **wrong** side. "Drat!" he said.

"It's going to be one of those days."

And he was right.

At breakfast he heard his parents arguing again.

They paid no attention to him. It was like he wasn't even there.

I might as well be a ghost, he thought.

At school, Tiger-Tiger

was picked last at games.

It hurt his feelings.

He felt

awful.

After school, his best friend decided to play with Zebra.

Tiger-Tiger felt rotten, as rotten as can be.

Everything was terrible.

Nobody cares, and nobody likes me.

Tiger-Tiger felt angry tears welling up in his eyes.

Suddenly there was a ripple in the water.

It was Turtle.

"What's up?" Turtle asked.

"Nothing," said Tiger-Tiger.

"Well, if *nothing* can make you cry, tell me more about this *nothing*. It must be very powerful."

"It's just that nobody cares," Tiger-Tiger sobbed. "Nobody likes me. Nobody cares if I'm around or not. Life is so unfair."

"Hmm," said Turtle. "You say that nobody cares about you and nobody likes you. Is that true? Are you sure?"

"Yes," said Tiger-Tiger. "My parents don't even know I'm around. Nobody likes me at school, and now my best friend is playing with Zebra!"

"That sounds pretty bad," Turtle said. "But **can you absolutely know it's true** that there is nobody in the whole wide world who cares about you or likes you?"

Tiger-Tiger thought about it and realized that he couldn't

be absolutely sure. "No, I can't. Not really," he said.

"So it's not true that nobody cares about

you or likes you. Right?" asked Turtle.

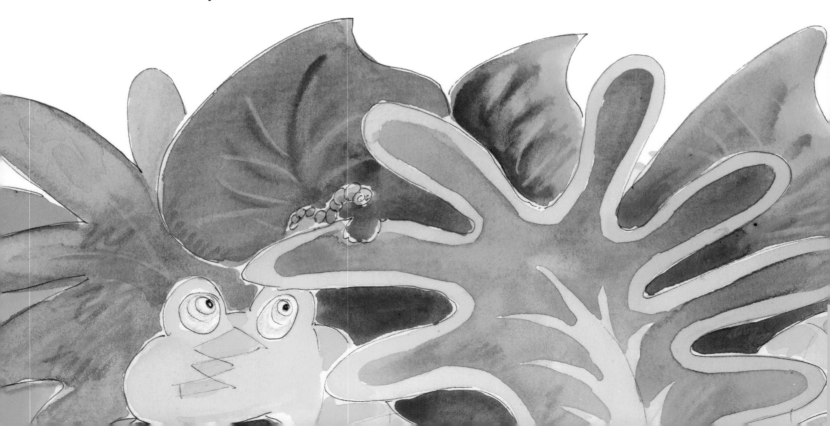

"How does it feel inside **you when you believe the thought** that nobody cares and nobody likes you?"

"I feel bad, lonely, and rotten," said Tiger-Tiger. "It makes me really sad."

"That must feel terrible," said Turtle. "Isn't it amazing what a little thought can do to you?"

"Now, **how does it feel if you are *not* thinking the thought** that nobody cares and nobody likes you? Who would you be if you could never believe that thought again?"

Tiger-Tiger's eyes brightened. "I would be a happy tiger! I would feel great! I could do anything, and nothing would bother me!"

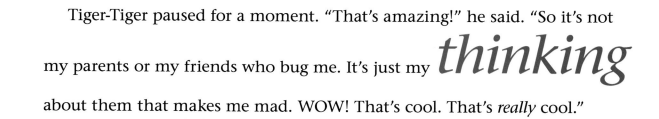

Tiger-Tiger paused for a moment. "That's amazing!" he said. "So it's not my parents or my friends who bug me. It's just my *thinking* about them that makes me mad. WOW! That's cool. That's *really* cool."

"You got it!" said Turtle. "It's your *thinking*. Now let's try something different. You think that nobody cares, and nobody likes you. Can you **turn** this thought **around?** I mean, can you find the opposite?"

Tiger-Tiger thought for a moment. "Like, <u>*Some*body *cares and likes me?*</u>"

"Yes," said Turtle. "Could that be true? Can you think of three examples of how your parents have shown you that they like you?"

Tiger-Tiger didn't have to think for long. "They never forget my birthday," he said. "They take me on great vacations. And they give me the **best hugs** in the world. They don't just care about me— they really *love* me."

"How about your best friend?" asked Turtle. "Can you find three examples with him?"

"Well, yes," said Tiger-Tiger. "He always saves a seat for me on the school bus. We are great game buddies. And he says he really likes to jam with me."

"And at school," Turtle asked, "is there anyone who likes you and cares about you?"

"I think my teacher likes me," said Tiger-Tiger. "She loves my drawings. And Rhino wants me to sit next to him at lunch. And Elephant always tells me secrets. I think she likes me a lot."

"Now find another **turnaround** for *Nobody cares, and nobody likes me*," Turtle said.

"Like, *I care, and I like everybody?*"

"That wouldn't be a bad idea, would it?" Turtle said with a smile. "And if it's not true for you now that you like *everybody*, how about *I care and like somebody?* I'm sure you can think of a lot of folks you like."

"Yes," Tiger-Tiger said. Then he thought for a moment and laughed. "I can think of another **turnaround**."

"You can?"

"Yes. How about *I care, and I like myself!*"

"Wow! That's the best of all!" Turtle said. "How would you do that?"

"I'll always find out if my bad thoughts are true or not. But I already know that they probably never are."

"Amazing how clever little tigers are these days," said Turtle.

We hope you enjoyed this Hay House book. If you'd like to receive our online catalog featuring additional information on Hay House books and products, or if you'd like to find out more about the Hay Foundation, please contact:

Hay House, Inc.
P.O. Box 5100
Carlsbad, CA 92018-5100

(760) 431-7695 or **(800) 654-5126**
(760) 431-6948 (fax) or **(800) 650-5115 (fax)**
www.hayhouse.com® • **www.hayfoundation.org**

***

Published and distributed in Australia by: Hay House Australia Pty. Ltd., 18/36 Ralph St., Alexandria NSW 2015 • *Phone:* 612-9669-4299 • *Fax:* 612-9669-4144 • www.hayhouse.com.au

Published and distributed in the United Kingdom by: Hay House UK, Ltd., Astley House, 33 Notting Hill Gate, London W11 3JQ
Phone: 44-20-3675-2450 • *Fax:* 44-20-3675-2451 • www.hayhouse.co.uk

Published and distributed in the Republic of South Africa by: Hay House SA (Pty), Ltd., P.O. Box 990, Witkoppen 2068 • *Phone/Fax:* 27-11-467-8904 • www.hayhouse.co.za

Published in India by: Hay House Publishers India, Muskaan Complex, Plot No. 3, B-2, Vasant Kunj, New Delhi 110 070 • *Phone:* 91-11-4176-1620 • *Fax:* 91-11-4176-1630 • www.hayhouse.co.in

Distributed in Canada by: Raincoast, 9050 Shaughnessy St., Vancouver, B.C. V6P 6E5
Phone: (604) 323-7100 • *Fax:* (604) 323-2600 • www.raincoast.com

***

<u>**Take Your Soul on a Vacation**</u>

Visit **www.HealYourLife.com**® to regroup, recharge, and reconnect with your own magnificence. Featuring blogs, mind-body-spirit news, and life-changing wisdom from Louise Hay and friends.

Visit **www.HealYourLife.com** today!